**W9-CBZ-107**

PECOS BILL

Tale retold by Bill Balcziak
Illustrated by Roberta Collier-Morales

Adviser: Dr. Alexa Sandmann, Professor of Literacy,
The University of Toledo; Member, International Reading Association

COMPASS POINT BOOKS
Minneapolis, Minnesota

Compass Point Books
3109 West 50th Street, #115
Minneapolis, MN 55410

Visit Compass Point Books on the Internet at *www.compasspointbooks.com*
or e-mail your request to *custserv@compasspointbooks.com*

Editor: Catherine Neitge
Designer: Les Tranby

Library of Congress Cataloging-in-Publication Data
Balcziak, Bill, 1962-
  Pecos Bill / written by Bill Balcziak ; illustrated by Roberta Collier-Morales.
      p. cm. — (The Imagination Series: Tall tales)
Summary: Presents the story of the baby Pecos Bill being raised by coyotes and his eventual marriage to
Slue-Foot Sue, another legend from the American Southwest.
  ISBN 0-7565-0460-0 (hardcover)
  1. Pecos Bill (Legendary character)—Legends. [1. Pecos Bill (Legendary character)—Legends. 2. Folklore—
United States. 3. Tall tales.] I. Title. II. Series.
  PZ8.1.B183 Pe 2003
  398.2'2'09764—dc21   2002015119

Table of Contents

Runaway Cattle

The townsfolk said you could hear the noise clear across the county. It started with a soft hum. It quickly grew into a roar. Within minutes, a giant cloud of dust could be seen rising in the east. It was a stampede! Thousands of longhorn cattle were loose and running wild.

The cowboys of the Lazy L Ranch had lost the longhorns near the town of Midland, Texas. Every cowboy knows longhorns are mean, sneaky, and fast. If you lose one during a cattle drive, it might be a year before you catch her. When 5,000 head of cattle get loose, well, you've got Texas-sized trouble.

The herd was racing toward Odessa, smashing everything in its path. It smashed houses, trees, and fences. It smashed *anything* in its way.

Folks from Midland sent frantic messages to Odessa to warn people to run for the hills. The telegraph poles were knocked down by the cattle, though, and the messages never made it. Hundreds of people were in danger.

What a Cowboy!

A few miles in front of the herd, a young man lay resting in the cool shade of a tall cactus. His name was Bill, but everybody called him Pecos Bill. He was known in those parts as the biggest, strongest, smartest cowboy who ever lived.

Pecos Bill felt the rumble made by the hooves of all those longhorns. He jumped up and saw the cloud of dust rising into the big Texas sky. Bill knew right away it was a stampede. He had to do something!

Pecos Bill leaped onto his horse, Widow-Maker, grabbed the reins, and headed for the dust cloud. They raced up a hill to get a better look. When Pecos Bill spotted the herd, he called "Giddyap" to Widow-Maker. They dashed down into the valley after the cattle. As they rode, Bill reached for his rope and formed a lasso. He twirled it faster and faster until it was as big around as a pasture. He raised it high over his head and threw it toward the rampaging herd. It snagged the lead animals and dropped neatly around the rest of the herd. Pecos Bill pulled the rope tight and yanked the reins to stop Widow-Maker.

Widow-Maker couldn't stop! She dug in her hooves, but the herd kept right on running toward the town. Now they were close enough to see the school. The stores along Main Street were coming into view.

Bill grabbed an even longer rope and formed another lasso with his free hand. He fed it out and snagged it on a high hill that stood over the valley. Pecos Bill held on tight. The herd pulled in one direction. The hill held its ground. Finally, when Bill thought for sure he would be torn in half, the herd came to a stop at the edge of town.

9

In the Beginning

Cowboys have enjoyed telling and retelling the story of Pecos Bill for more than 100 years.

The story begins when Bill was a not-so-tiny baby. He grew fast on a diet of milk, tumbleweeds, cactus, and hot Texas barbecue. By the time he was six months old, he could ride a horse and rope a calf. His hands were so strong he could bring his father, Pecos Johnny, to his knees with one squeeze of his pa's big toe.

Bill's parents, Pecos Johnny and Pecos Annie, made a good life for their baby. When Bill was nearing his first birthday, however, the family decided to move away.

"Too many people in these parts," said Pecos Annie, even though the nearest neighbor was 50 miles (80 kilometers) away.

"Too crowded around here," said Pecos Johnny, even though the nearest town was 100 miles (161 kilometers) away. So they loaded Bill into a crib on the back of the wagon. They hitched up the horses, Pecos Nellie and Pecos King, and drove off into the wilderness.

The first night on the trail, Pecos Johnny and Pecos Annie looked for a good place to bunk down. A storm was brewing, and it was hard to see. So they pulled their hats down tight and pointed the horses into the storm. "Make a run for it, Pecos Johnny," cried his wife.

The wagon bounced along the rough trail, and the crib flew out the back. Pecos Bill was still inside, hanging on for dear life.

The storm was upon them now. Pecos Johnny and Pecos Annie had no idea they had lost their sweet son. They kept driving as fast as they could to find shelter. That was the last they saw of Bill for a long, long time.

Meanwhile, Pecos Bill was in trouble. When his crib left the wagon, it tumbled along the trail until it came to rest upside down in a ditch. The child was trapped! Pecos Bill started to cry, but the sound could not be heard above the wind and rain and thunder.

Bill pulled on the bars of the crib, but even with his great strength, he could not free himself.

All hope was lost for the poor boy until a sudden bolt of lightning shot through the sky. During that brief moment, a wet, wandering family of coyotes saw the crib and stopped to look. The mother coyote saw little Pecos Bill crying inside the upside-down crib and wanted to help.

She and the father coyote grabbed the crib with their strong jaws and pulled until it turned over with a crash. The mother coyote gently lifted Pecos Bill by his diaper and carried him back to their home in a nearby cave. He quickly warmed up and fell asleep, snug in a big snoring mound of fur.

Living with the Coyotes

The coyotes did a fine job of raising Pecos Bill as their own. They taught him to hunt and gather food. His coyote brothers and sisters teased him and showed him how to fight and play. He grew fast, and in no time at all he was a big, normal, happy teen. A teen who happened to be raised by coyotes, of course.

One day the coyote family, including Pecos Bill, was swimming in a nearby stream. Overhead, a hawk circled lazy figure-eights in the clear blue sky. Much to their surprise, a man rode by on a horse. He stared in amazement at the sight of the boy swimming with the coyotes.

"Hey, there!" cried the man. "What's going on down there?"

Everyone jumped from the water and ran for the cave. Everyone, that is, except Pecos Bill. For some reason he didn't run or hide. He just floated in the water, looking at the man.

"Are you OK, son?" asked the man.

"Guuuh, uhhhh," said Pecos Bill. It was the first time he'd tried to talk to somebody since he was a baby. He wasn't sure what to say. "Gaahh, flaah," he said.

The man walked down to the stream and pulled the boy from the water. He put an arm around Pecos Bill and said, "We better get you home, young fella. Your ma and pa must be missing you."

Bill smiled at the man and said, "Maaaaah, paaaaah."

Bill waved good-bye to his coyote family and the pair rode off together to a nearby town. The legend of "The Young Man Who Was Raised by Coyotes" spread like a prairie fire. People from across Texas came to see Pecos Bill in person.

Among the many visitors were several teachers who spent hours with the boy teaching him reading, writing, and arithmetic.

After a few months, Pecos Bill could talk, read, and figure numbers like anyone his age. The owner of the Big R Ranch asked Pecos Bill what he wanted to do with his life.

"I dunno," said the boy.

"Well then," said the rancher. "Why don't come out to the ranch and learn to be a cowboy?"

Pecos Bill nearly jumped out of his boots at the idea. "Yes, sirree!" he said. "I'm going to be a cowboy!

The Best Cowboy Ever

Pecos Bill became the best cowboy the state of Texas had ever seen. He was faster than a mountain stream and quick as a hungry snake. He could rope a steer a half-mile away and break a horse with a dirty look.

People said he rode a mountain lion into town just to see the look on their faces. When a cyclone bore down on the Big R Ranch, he lassoed it and dragged it to the Gulf of Mexico where it drifted out to sea.

21

The Girl of His Dreams

Every gal in the county wanted to be Pecos Bill's girlfriend. Bill didn't pay any attention, however, until he met one very special young lady on a hot, dusty afternoon. Pecos Bill just happened to be swimming in the same stream where he was found by the kindly man. He was floating on his back, enjoying the quiet, when the water exploded around him.

"Nah," said Pecos Bill, staring. "It just can't be." He rubbed his eyes and looked again. Sure enough, there was a beautiful girl riding a catfish the size of a cow. The girl laughed and waved at Bill. She disappeared with a wink around a bend in the stream. Bill swam after her. "Wait!" he yelled, but it was no use. The cowgirl was gone, and Pecos Bill was in love.

23

The girl's name was Slue-Foot Sue. She was smart, funny, and as tough as cowhide. She could ride a horse, rope a calf, brand a bull, and still look as pretty as a cactus flower in the morning dew.

One day soon after, Slue-Foot Sue saw Pecos Bill riding through town. She smiled and asked if she could ride his horse. "Gee whiz, Sue," he said. "The Widow-Maker won't let anybody ride her 'cept me."

Sue decided to tease him. "Why, Pecos, don't you think little ol' me could handle Widow-Maker?" she said.

"Sure, I'll let you ride her, Sue," laughed Pecos Bill, "as long as you marry me first!"

They were married that very day. As soon as the ceremony was over, Sue jumped in Widow-Maker's saddle and the horse started to buck. Slue-Foot Sue grabbed the reins as tight as she could, but Widow-Maker was determined to throw her off. They jerked around and around the town.

Finally Widow-Maker bucked so hard, Sue was thrown into the sky. She sailed so high that everyone lost sight of her.

When she finally came down a few minutes later, she landed right back on Widow-Maker's saddle.

"Hoooo-wheeeee" she yelled, and the horse threw her up into the air again. Each time Slue-Foot Sue landed, Widow-Maker got madder and madder, sending her higher and higher into the air. She kept bouncing and bouncing until she landed square on her bustle. This time Sue shot so high in the sky she circled the moon!

Up and down she went until Pecos Bill decided he'd seen enough. He played out his rope and threw a lasso right around his new bride's shoulders. "Here you go, darlin'," he called, and pulled her gently back down into his arms.

Their wedding day was the last anybody saw of Pecos Bill and Slue-Foot Sue. Later, some folks heard the couple had been riding Widow-Maker atop Pikes Peak. Others say they heard Bill tamed a volcano with his lasso.

Most people, though, think Pecos Bill finally met up with his ma and pa somewhere in the western desert. Of course it was far, far away from anybody else. There, they say, is where Pecos Bill and Slue-Foot Sue settled down to raise their family and live out their long, happy lives.

The Adventures of Pecos Bill

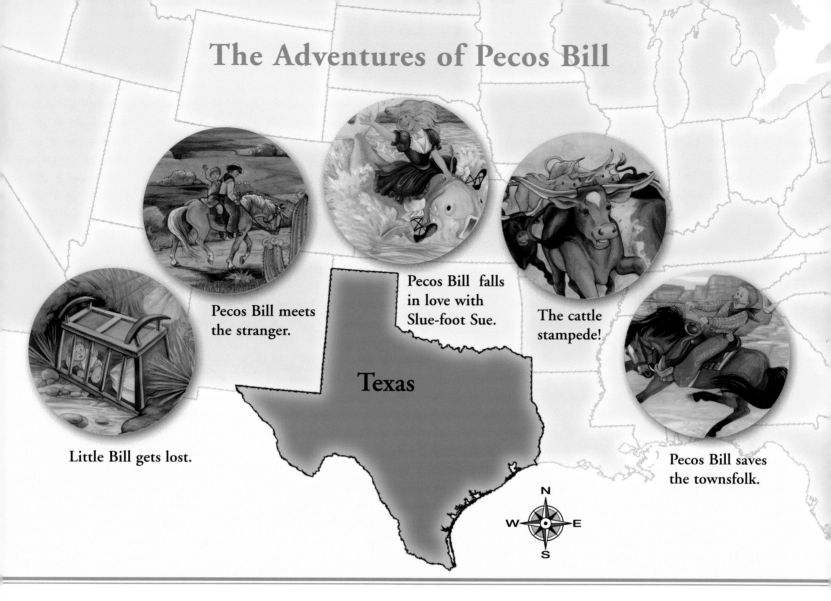

Little Bill gets lost.

Pecos Bill meets the stranger.

Pecos Bill falls in love with Slue-foot Sue.

Texas

The cattle stampede!

Pecos Bill saves the townsfolk.

The story of Pecos Bill is as big and wild as the state of Texas. It all started when cowboys of the Old West gathered around the campfire. They would relax after a hard day's work by telling stories, each one bigger and bolder than the others. It was an easy way to pass the time, and it created some amazing characters. One of those tall tales was about a cowboy named Pecos

Bill. It started as a contest among the cowboys. They dared each other to imagine the greatest cowboy who ever lived. Over the years, the legend of Pecos Bill grew bigger and bigger until it became a part of Texas itself. Now, wherever people go in Texas, they're sure to hear about Pecos Bill, his wife, Slue-Foot Sue, and their horse, Widow-Maker.

Cowboy Caviar

Who would want real caviar when you can enjoy the cowboy version instead? You know all about real caviar, don't you? Fish eggs! Cowboy Caviar is more like a fancy bean dip. This recipe makes about twelve servings.

1 can (15 oz.) black beans, rinsed & drained
1 can (4 oz.) chopped ripe olives, drained
1 small onion, finely chopped (about 1/4 cup)
1 clove garlic, finely chopped
2 tablespoons vegetable oil
2 tablespoons lime juice
1/4 teaspoon salt

1/8 teaspoon crushed red pepper
1/4 teaspoon ground cumin
1/8 teaspoon pepper
1 package (8 oz.) cream cheese, softened
2 hard cooked eggs, peeled and chopped
1 green onion with top, sliced

Mix all the ingredients except cream cheese, eggs and onions. Cover and refrigerate for at least two hours. Spread the cream cheese on a serving plate. Spoon the bean mixture evenly over the cream cheese. Put the eggs on the beans around the edge of the plate. Sprinkle with green onion. Serve with tortilla chips.

Glossary

amazement—great surprise or wonder

barbecue—meat cooked on a grill and covered in spicy sauce

bustle—a pad that makes the back of a woman's skirt look bigger

cactus—a plant with spines that grows in dry, hot areas

ceremony—an important formal event, like a wedding

cyclone—a storm with very strong winds

determined—firm in sticking to a purpose

frantic—excited by worry or fear

lasso—a rope formed into a loop; a cowboy uses a lasso to catch an animal

legend—a story passed down through the years that may not be completely true

longhorn cattle—a type of cattle with very long horns

rampaging—rushing wildly about

stampede—a sudden, wild running of a frightened group of animals

telegraph—a way to send messages over long distances by wire; telegraph was used in the 1800s.

twirl—to spin around quickly

tumbleweeds—plants that break away from their roots and roll across the land, pushed along by the wind

Did You Know?

★ The first story of Pecos Bill, called "Saga of Pecos Bill," was written in 1923 by Edward O'Reilly.

★ Pecos Bill "starred" in two movies:

Melody Time and *Tall Tale: The Unbelievable Adventures of Pecos Bill.*

★ Pecos Bill appeared on a 32-cent United States postage stamp in 1996.

Want to Know More?

At the Library

Kellogg, Steven. *Pecos Bill.* New York: William Morrow and Co., 1986.

Osborne, Mary Pope. *American Tall Tales.* New York: Scholastic, 1991.

Spies, Karen. *Our Folk Heroes.* Brookfield, Conn.: The Millbrook Press, 1994.

Stoutenburg, Adrien. *American Tall Tales.* New York: Puffin Books, 1976.

On the Web

Diamond R Ranch
http://www.nationalcowboymuseum.org/diamondr/index.html
To visit a fun interactive web site hosted by the National Cowboy and Western Heritage Museum

Institute of Texan Cultures Kids Stuff
http://www.texancultures.utsa.edu/kidsstuff/kidssplash/kidssplash.htm
To learn about Texas history in this "just for kids" web site

Texas Beyond History
http://www.texasbeyondhistory.net/index.htm
Click on Kids Only? to start digging through Texas history

Through the Mail

National Cowgirl Museum and Hall of Fame
1720 Gendy Street
Fort Worth, Texas 76107
817/336-4475
To write for information on this museum that honors remarkable women

On the Road

West of the Pecos Museum
Highway 285 and First Street
Pecos, Texas 79772
915/445-5076
To visit an interesting museum housed in the former Orient Hotel and Saloon

Index

About the Author
Bill Balcziak has written a number of books for children. When he is
not writing, he enjoys going to plays, movies, and museums. Bill lives
in Minnesota with his family under the shadow of Paul Bunyan and
Babe, the Blue Ox.

About the Illustrator
Roberta Collier-Morales has been a professional illustrator since 1979.
She graduated from Colorado State University and received a master's
degree from Marywood University in Pennsylvania. She lives in Boulder,
Colorado.